A MIGHTY
SMILING
FIREFLY
JOSLIN
FITZGERALD

This lovely, guiding book is dedicated to my new, beautiful Granddaughter Aria. My Sweetheart, it is my desire that you will always know how much I love you! And even though we may not be able to be together all the time. May you always find the nice, life lessons written in all my stories a way to bring magic and happiness into your life! So, knowing that you will always Fit-In.. no matter what you are doing! Please realize, since you are a Part of me... that we are just ALIKE! And being a Part of my Heart, when you see YOUR SMILE in the mirror, just know that is MY SMILE, SMILING BACK AT YOU ALL THE TIME! Likewise know, like an ARIA song, that you sing all day long, I will ALWAYS BE RIGHT BY YOUR SIDE! That means, every time you hear OUR voice, see OUR FACE, or read my books. You will know that I will always be a sweet part of your life, SONG, and heart. So, wanting you to find your Happily Ever After, that will always bring you happiness also laughter. Giving You My Voice... to sing OUR songs... All my life, in Some-way... I promise to gift you with Smiles. Hearts. Love. Songs. Kisses, Prayers, and Hugs, all day and night long!

Love Forever from me to you, morning to evening! Your Merry Mary Mimi...

WHY DON'T WE FIT IN WITH OUR FRIENDS?
The Place Of Candy Ice Cream and Cakes

Once-upon-a-time in an Out-of-Sight place that was full of nice Candy, Ice Cream, and Cakes. Two Striped Fireflies named Mighty Mike and Star Shine were playing. And flying beside Cherry Ice Cream Moonbeams, living in a cool space where everyone Smiled all the time. Life was Merry in the LAND OF BEING ALIKE. But WAIT! Not everything was fine! Because being Striped, and NOT looking like the other Gold Fireflies. Having an odd light… Some THING in the kid's life was not quite right!

That means, rising high, glowing low, floating like colorful Striped Lights in the sky wherever they would go. Never Fitting-In with their glowing gold friend's, life was weird for Mighty Mike, and Star Shine, since they had odd, shiny rear ends. So, being Striped while living in the LAND OF BEING ALIKE Mighty Mike and Star Shine did not feel alright. And Not looking like the Gold Fireflies, who had yellow glows. On Low Light Nights, things were not quite right for Star Shine, or Mighty Mike.

That's why, living in the LAND OF BEING ALIKE, Star Shine and Mighty Mike found it hard to Smile. Because Upset with their lives they were Not content with their Weird looking Rear Ends! Bottom line, looking like Stripes, the kids were not like the other Fireflies with the gold glowing lights. So since they had different Bottom Lines even as the kids tried to Smile all the time. From the beginning, Mighty Mike and Star Shine felt strangely out of place since they never Fit-In with their friends!

I WISH WE FIT IN WITH OUR FRIENDS!

But Wait, that was kind-of-Okay. Because knowing their sweet Striped lights were Guiding Signs. The kids agreed being Special, and Strange, might come in handy if they lost their way. That's why, on low light nights, when they felt out of place. Since they did not Fit-In with their Gold friends. The kids realized if they lost their Smiles, their Striped Lights would show them the way to go Home again. And that was nice to know, in case they left the homey Place of the gold also yellow glows.

So, seeing their Striped lights in a strange way. Mighty Mike and Star Shine agreed if things did not work out right someday. They would need a Guiding Sign to bring them back to their LAND OF BEING ALIKE. Bottom line, trying to Fit-In somewhere new if they went over the Merry Cherry Ice Cream Moon, looking for a cooler life. They both realized If they changed their mind, about what they wished to find. To come Home, and find their Smile, they would need some STAR LIGHT... and BRIGHT MULTICOLORED SIGNS!

That's when, Mike said. "Star Shine If we can't find our Smile one day. And we decide to roam far away. We must be able to return to our Merry Cherry Moon. That's why, trying to find the ALIKE-Life where we Fit-In, if we see Leaving Home was a Big Mistake! One of us needs to stay behind, in the place of Ice Cream, Candy, and Cakes! So, to find our Smile. ONE of us needs to SHINE, as a Guiding COME HOME LIGHT SIGN, all the time! In case we don't like... what we try to find on the OTHER SIDE!

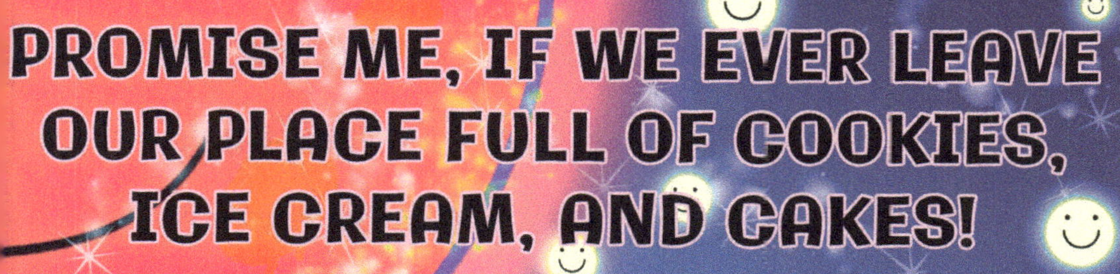
PROMISE ME, IF WE EVER LEAVE
OUR PLACE FULL OF COOKIES,
ICE CREAM, AND CAKES!

THAT ONE OF US WILL
STAY BEHIND TO
SHINE OUR NEVER
ENDING GUIDING
LIGHT OF LOVE INTO
THE SKY, SO WE CAN
GO HOME AGAIN!

Next, Star Shine replied." So, let's Promise each other, no matter which one goes far away. To return soon to our Cool Merry Cherry Moon, that one of us will stay behind in the place of Ice Cream, Candy, and Cakes. That way, IF we find our Smile has been Waiting for us inside the LAND OF BEING ALIKE. To see our family and friends again. By following our Bright, glowing Star Light, and SIGNS of LOVE from Above. We will Both make sure that the Other one of us, can go back HOME!

So, knowing if they lost their Smile one day and one of them roamed far away, they would need a grand plan to Fit-In better with their Gold Friends. Trying to make life be what they wanted it to be again. Mike, and Star Shine promised if they LOST their Smile, they would be there for one another no matter where they roamed over the miles. So, realizing there would be a way to Go Back Home. Life was fine all the time. Until one dark lonely Night when things were Not Quite Alright!

Bottom line, nice time was fine. UNTIL one DARK NIGHT when everything Switched in the LAND OF BEING ALIKE. So, living below the Ice Cream Moonbeams shining like Stripes all the time. Always Unable to Fit-In since he had a weird looking glow and a different rear end! Mike finally GAVE UP on being ALIKE! That's when, overnight knowing he would never be LIKE his glowing Gold Firefly Friends, since his Bottom line did NOT FIT-IN! Having a Low Light Night, Mighty Mike LOST HIS SMILE!

And LOSING HIS SMILE on that Low Light Night, Mike realized growing up Strange, he had never LIKED living in their yellow, blue, and gold place. That's why, being Striped and not being the same, Mighty Mike LOST HIS SMILE ONE DARK NIGHT! Then unable to Fit-In, that's also when... Mike decided, even though he liked his Candy, Ice cream and Cake. That Glowing like a nice Striped firefly, when everyone else was Gold with a Yellow light, that being Different, might not be quite as nice!

That's when tired of feeling strangely out of place, one day when things were not quite right, Mike said. "Star Shine, I want to see the latest Exciting Sights on the Other Side! And as, I visit the Lands of Ties-Pies-Kites-also-Butterflies. I want to find out if I might Fit-In living in a new place! That's why, I need to say Bye Bye... to my Candy, Ice Cream and Cakes! Because I think life will be cooler living where things are NOT yellow, or gold too! Then I will not be in such a Rude Crude Mood!"

I WANT TO GO
TO THE LAND OF
TIES, PIES, KITES,
and BUTTERFLIES!

So, tired of NOT BEING ALIKE, because he never Fit-In! Mike went Over the Merry Cherry Ice Cream Moonbeams, searching for his New COOLER ALIKE friends. And leaving home Mike went far away! Yes, that seemed like a Grand Plan for Mighty Mike in many ways. But WAIT! Trying to see things in a different Light. Right after Mike Lost his Smile. When Mike left home. Nothing was nice for Star Shine! Because, left behind, with NO ALIKE GLOW, now crying, Striped Star Shine, was all ALONE!

But wait NOT WANTING TO BE ALONE! Star Shine realized it was a MATTER OF TIME before Mike would CHANGE HIS MIND! Then, he would SEE... that his Fit-In Place, had always been waiting in the land of Candy, Ice Cream and Cakes. That's when, Star Shine realized IF SHE TURNED HER STRIPED LIGHT ON HIGH. Mike would find his Smile in a Land of Being ALIKE! So, knowing he would Return again! Star Shine let Mike Leave the Merry Cherry Moonbeams behind, to find his new friends!

Now, that seemed like the End of things. But instead that was the Beginning of a SEEING-THE-LIGHT Journey. Because as Mike left her behind even as she started crying that was the time when Star Shine turned her BRIGHT, STRIPED LIGHT on HIGH for Mighty Mike! And wanting her brother to COME HOME AGAIN! Knowing LOVE WOULD BE THEIR GUIDE. That's why, Star Shine TURNED ON HER LOVELY MULTICOLORED LIGHT after sending Mighty Mike far away with extra Kisses, Hugs and Star SIGNS!

MIGHTY MIKE NEEDS TO FIND THE LIGHT
COME HOME SOON

So, realizing, Mike needed to find out things were NOT better in the Land of Ties-Pies-Kites-and-Butterflies. For Mike to realize his Rightful place had always been where he Fit-In with his Gold Friends. Star Shine kept her Striped LIGHT on HIGH! And keeping her Promise to him, while putting up a COME HOME SOON SIGN that looked like A BRIGHT GLOWING STAR! Shining her Guiding STARLIGHT in the sky all the time. Needing to SEE the light. Star Shine let Mike go off to Find his Smile!

So, trying to Fit-In, while wanting to find his Smile somewhere new. Knowing his sisters HELLO STAR SHINE LIGHT would be there to guide him home. In that clue, Mike felt alright going off alone. And chasing a restless wind trying to find a new beginning, Mighty Mike left Star-Shine behind! Next, following the Signs-of-Life that sent him Over the Ice Cream Moon. Mighty Mike roamed low and high. And one of the Cool places Mighty Mike found himself going to was, the Land-of-Ties.

That's why, trying to find a new ALIKE Place in the Land-of-Ties, Mike felt like he would Fit-In with a new group of family and friends over night. But NOT looking like a TIE! Mike realized the Land-of-Ties, was not Right for him. So, going Over a Balloon Shaped Moon. Mike did not Fit-In... inside the LAND-OF-TIES! That means, in a Tied-up land, where everyone looked like Bow Ties. Thin Ties. Neck Ties, also Fat Ties. A lost, alone, misguided Firefly did not find his Smile, in the Land-of-Ties.

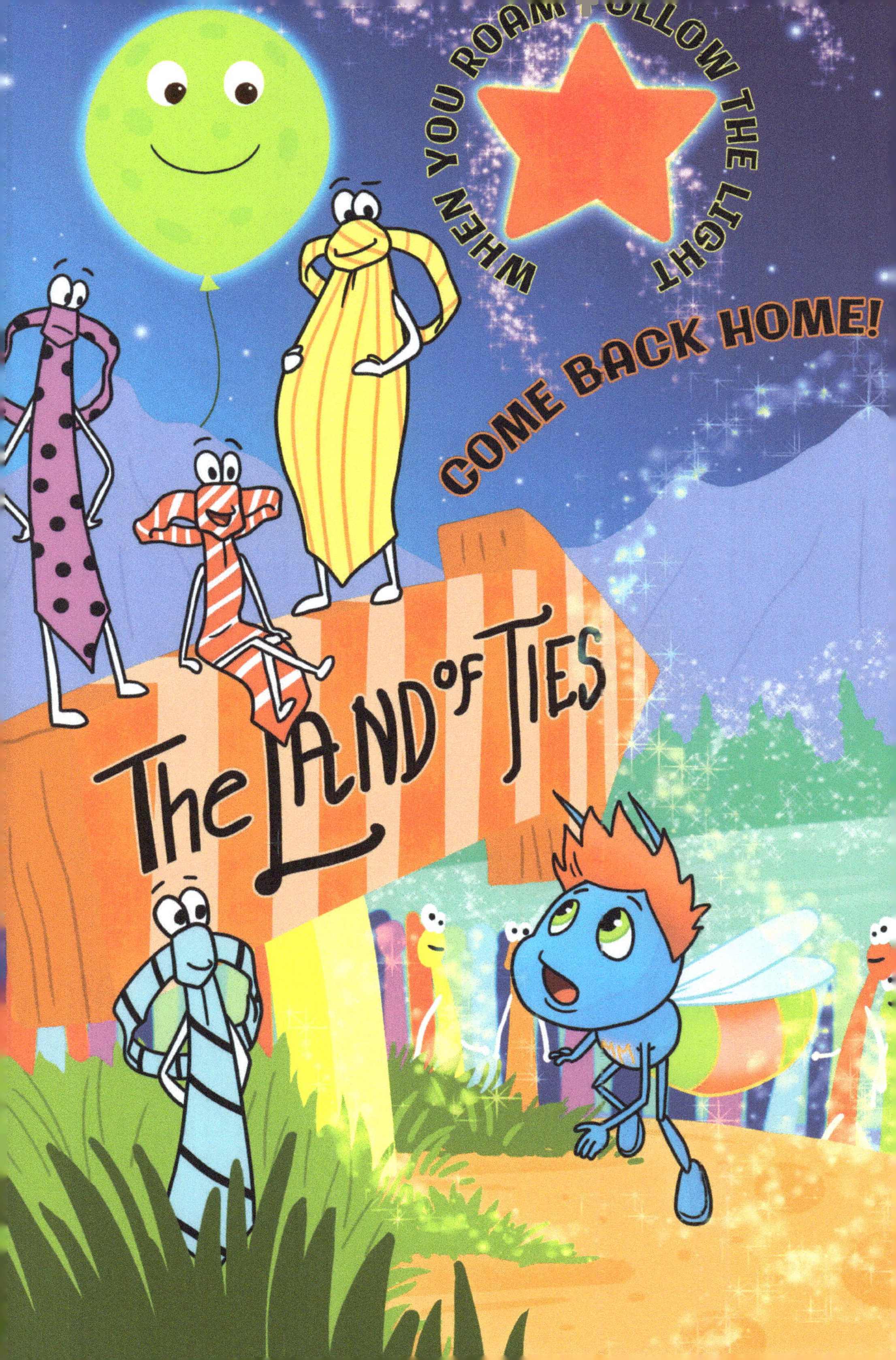

WHEN YOU ROAM FOLLOW THE LIGHT
COME BACK HOME!
The LAND of TIES

And, in that discovery, it was also in the Land-of-Ties, Mike realized it was LOVE, Not Color or Size that Tied people together! So, knowing he broke his Tie to Star Shine, that made Mighty Mike cry! Even so, Mike felt like things might be better going over a cool Hooting Moon! So, knowing Star Shine's ALIKE light would guide him home. Mike kept roaming! And that made life nice and fine! But WAIT! That's not Right! Because, nothing was nice after Mike left his friends, also sister behind!

That's why, even though Mike left Star Shine, and the nice Gold Fireflies. Mike was glad to realize if things did not work out right in the exciting Lands of Ties-Pies-Kites-and-Butterflies he could go home anytime! Bottom line, Mike realized one day or night that Star Shine's Striped light would Guide him back to the yellow, also gold fireflies. So, closing another NOT Right door. Mike kept going Away from the light! And to find his Smile Mike left the nice Land-of-Ties, heading to the Land-of-Pies!

So, trying to find an ALIKE Place in the Land-of-Pies, Mike felt like he would Fit-In with a new group of family and cool friends over night. But NOT looking like a Pie. Mike realized the Land-of-Pies, was not Right for his life. And, not Fitting-In going over a new Hooting Moon in an UNLIKE land where everyone looked like Pumpkin Pies. Cherry pies. Lemon Pies. And Blueberry Pies too. Mike realized a misguided, alone, sad, Striped, CLUELESS Firefly would not find his Smile in the Land-of-Pies.

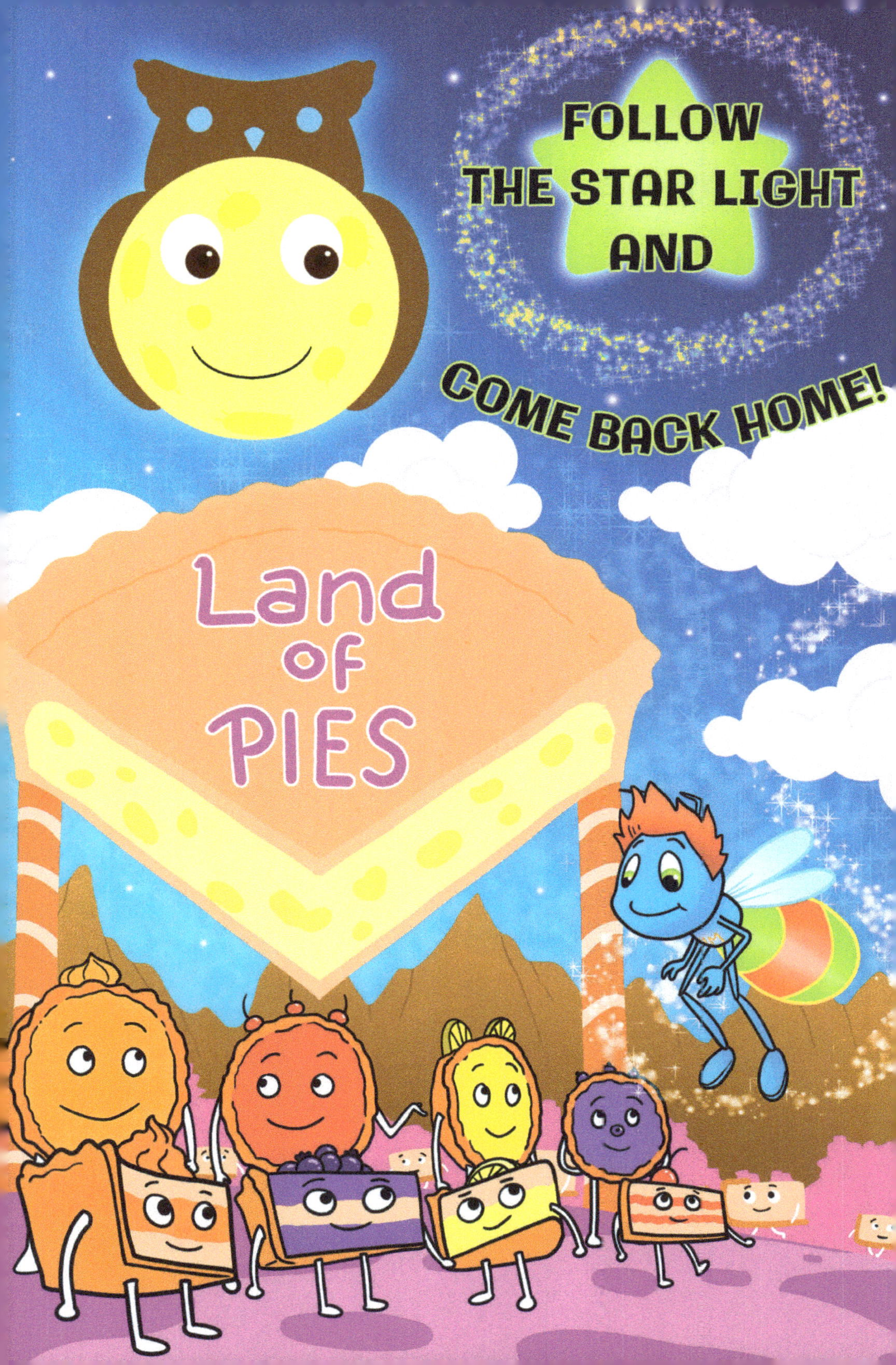
FOLLOW THE STAR LIGHT AND
COME BACK HOME!
Land
OF
PIES

Next, it was there in the Land-of-Pies, Mighty Mike realized life would always be bittersweet. Because even though a Pie was nice. The longer a Pie stayed in the light and heat it would sour, smell terrible, and grow Stinky mold, as it got old. That's when, Mighty Mike realized, not finding his Home in the Hooting Moon Light. Time in the Strange Lands-of-Pies would NOT be Alright for a Striped Firefly. And that lost idea, made Mike miss his Candy, Cakes, Ice Cream, also Star Shine!

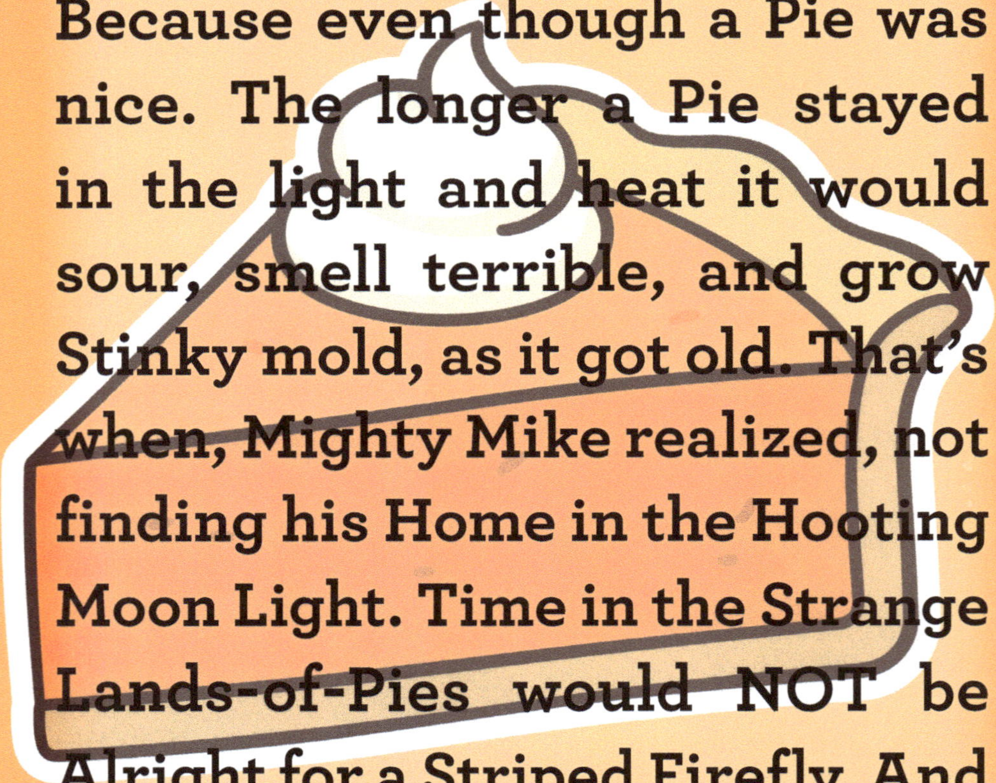

And missing her Smile, also brother Star Shine felt the same Sad way about things. That's why, knowing her best friend was lost and alone. Lonesome Star Shine kept GLOWING! So, true to her Return Promise Star Shine kept her GUIDING STAR SIGN ON HIGH all the time! And using her Bright Light to mark their shiny Golden Road! Star Shine kept searching the sky for Mike's bold roaming Striped glow. Because, she realized LOVE, and Friends would bring her brother's Smile back Home again!

WHEN YOU ROAM AND LIVE FAR AWAY... LOVE, FAMILY, AND FRIENDS WILL ALWAYS BRING YOU HOME AGAIN!

But on the other side of time NEVER SEEING THE LIGHT. Even though things were NOT nice for Mighty Mike in the land of Ties, also Pies. Still looking for his Smile. Mighty Mike was not ready to go back Home to Star Shine, or return to the yellow, likewise ALIKE skies. Because day and night, unable to Fit-In with his Gold Friends. Trying to find his New Group, after going Over the Balloon, and now Owl shaped Hooting Moon. Mike had not yet put together all his new, cool GO HOME CLUES!

So, knowing Nice Star Shine's Glow could guide him home, Mike kept roaming. And on the Hooting Side of the Moon, Mike was Happy to realize if things did not work out in the Land-of-Ties-Pies-Kites-and-Butterflies. One day Star Shine's nice Bright Striped Sign Light, would Guide him back Home to his Candy, Ice Cream, and Cake. Therefore, keeping their family Promise Star Shine remained behind to make sure that things were Alright! And to find his Smile, Mike headed off to the Land-of-Kites!

That's why, leaving the Land-of-Pies, trying to find his home roaming low likewise high, Mike kept looking for a better ALIKE life. So, wanting to Fit-In somewhere else by trying to Find his Smile. On his way to the Land-of-Kites Mike went over a Spoon Moon. And roaming far away from his home trying to Fit-In, going over a new Cool Moon that looked like a Spoon. By following the Strange Signs that sent him away from his LAND OF BEING ALIKE, Mike took an odd ride and Mighty flight in life.

So, trying to find an ALIKE Place in the Land-of-Kites, Mike felt like he would Fit-In with a new group of family and friends over night. But NOT looking like a Kite, Mighty Mike realized the Land-of-Kites was not right for him. And not Fitting-In going Over a Spoon Moon. In a new land where everyone looked like Tall Kites. Long Kites. Strong Kites. And Small Kites. It was clear a lost, CLUELESS, alone, and misguided, Striped Firefly would not find his Smile, waiting in the Land-of-Kites.

FOLLOW THE CLUES AND COME HOME SOON!
Land of Kites

Next it was in the nice Land-of-Kites sadly Mighty Mike verified that Kites could let go. So, seeing the Kites floating away into the dark of the night that made Mike feel even more alone. And being really lonely, Mighty Mike started to miss Home! Bottom line, Unable to find his Smile, or Fit-In, Mike realized NOTHING on the Other-Side, was going Right for him! So, wanting to go home again. Mike started to Miss his Candy, Cakes, Ice Cream, also Star Shine, and his glowing gold friends!

But WAIT! There was one more Land Mike needed to visit! So still trying to FIND HIS SMILE, while looking for nicer friends, Mike left the UNLIKE Kites behind. And to live with the Butterflies, Mike went over a cool Moon that looked like a Flower Blooming. But not looking like a Tiny Butterfly. Spying Butterfly. Shy Butterfly. Or Exercising Butterfly. Knowing Butterflies could likewise fly away, and not make it home safely. Mike realized he would never Fit-In living in any of those odd places!

FOLLOW THE
NEW CLUES AND
COME HOME SOON!
Land of Butterflies

So, it was in the UNLIKE Land-of-Butterflies where LIFE and TIME CHANGED! Because it was on a new LOW-LIGHT-NIGHT, when Mike realized that he missed his Cool Merry Cherry Moon! He also missed the Gold Fireflies too! And, knowing nothing was Right, since he left his Mother, Father, Brother, Sister, and Friends Crying! Mike finally realized TO FIT-IN... it WAS TIME for him, TO GO HOME again, to his LAND OF BEING ALIKE! That's when, Mike realized he needed to FIND HIS SMILE where he left it behind!

I AM GOING HOME!
TO THE LAND OF
BEING ALIKE!
Of Candy
and Cakes

Bottom line, finally Mighty Mike realized the only Time that ever made him SMILE. Was where he could be himself flying around with his family, while he enjoyed playing with his nice kind, gold friends in Cool Merry Cherry Moonlight. And that's when Mike realized if he was ever going Fit-In! That he needed to find his SMILE where he LEFT IT behind with Star Shine, his Family, and his gold FRIENDS! So, following an orange glowing moon that looked like Fruit! Mike wanted to GO HOME SOON!

That's when needing to SEE the Light! Realizing he would never Fit-In-living in the UN-ALIKE Lands-of-Ties-Pies-Kites-or-Butterflies. To find his Smile Mighty Mike said GOODBYE to those he did not know. And searching the nighttime sky. Mighty Mike Followed Star Shine's glowing LIGHT day and night! Bottom line, to FIND HIS SMILE. Mike left the Balloon, Hooting, Spoon, Blooming, and Fruit Shaped Moons behind. And Chasing Star Shine's Guiding Glow, Mighty Mike finally went Home!

GOODBYE TO THE LAND OF CRY'S
GOODBYE TO THE LAND OF SIGHS
GOODBYE TO THE LAND OF PIES
GOODBYE TO THE LAND OF TIES
GOODBYE TO THE LAND OF KITES
GOODBYE TO THE LAND OF BUTTERFLIES.
AND HELLO TO THE LAND OF CANDY, COOKIES, CAKES, BEING ALIKE, &
SMILES!

So, realizing that he HAD always FIT-IN with his Family, and Gold Friends. Finding his Smile was waiting for him. Mike, returned to the ones he LOVED! And as, Mike left the Balloon, Hooting, Spoon, Blooming, and nice Fruit Shaped Moons behind he could SEE he did NOT need to live in the land of TIES-PIES-KITES-AND BUTTERFLIES to be ALIKE! And that was Cool news! Because as Mighty Mike found his LIGHT INSIDE! Mike realized even though he was Different on the Outside! HIS SMILE would let him FIT-IN day or night! And just like that Mighty Mike SAW THE LIGHT!

MIGHTY MIKE HAS FINALLY SEEN THE LIGHT!

Next, as Star Shine spied Mike's Striped glow in the sky she finally stopped crying! And that was nice. Because when Star Shine WELCOMED HER BROTHER HOME, they realized... BEING DIFFERENT WAS THE SAME AS BEING ALIKE!!! So, FINDING their NEVER-ENDING SMILES! The two kids happily FIT-IN below the Merry Cherry Moonlight! And knowing WHAT HE LEFT BEHIND... WAS WHAT THEY NEEDED TO FIND life was Alright! Because SEEING that they would always be Different on the Outside. They knew... it was Love for One Another that made them ALIKE INSIDE!

And as, the kind Gold Fireflies WELCOMED Mighty Mike BACK HOME TO THE LAND OF BEING ALIKE. His nice ALIKE Friends started Celebrating with him! That's when EVERYBODY FOUND A MIGHTY GREAT PLACE WHERE THEY ALL FIT-IN! And in that Delightful News... Mike realized TO BE MIGHTY HAPPY. AND TO HAVE A MIGHTY SMILE. HE NEEDED TO LOVE HIMSELF THE WAY HE WAS ALL THE TIME! Because Being MIGHTY and ALIKE ON THE INSIDE WAS THE RIGHT WAY to enjoy life! That's when finding How he was ALIKE, Mike turned into a Mighty BRIGHT, Mighty Mike!

I AM SO GLAD THAT YOU FOUND YOUR SMILE.

So, the Moral-To-The-Story is this. Fitting-In, will never be easy. But Fitting-In, will get easier when YOU are Excited about WHO YOU ARE! That's why, LIKING WHO YOU ARE INSIDE FROM THE START! To Fit-In, You must realize that being Different around family also friends will be alright! And that's good, INSIDE, ALIKE advice! Because everybody will always be slightly strange, in their own weird, nice ways! That's why, SHINING differently all the time! Being MIGHTY Happy on the INSIDE. Glowing in your own way. You will always FIT-IN on the Outside night and day. And seeing the Light shining in your sky, through your eyes... that's also when you will find your ALIKE Place in Life. Bottom line, knowing that you FIT-IN all the time. When you are MIGHTY, and ALIKE INSIDE! That's when, you will find your SMILE.

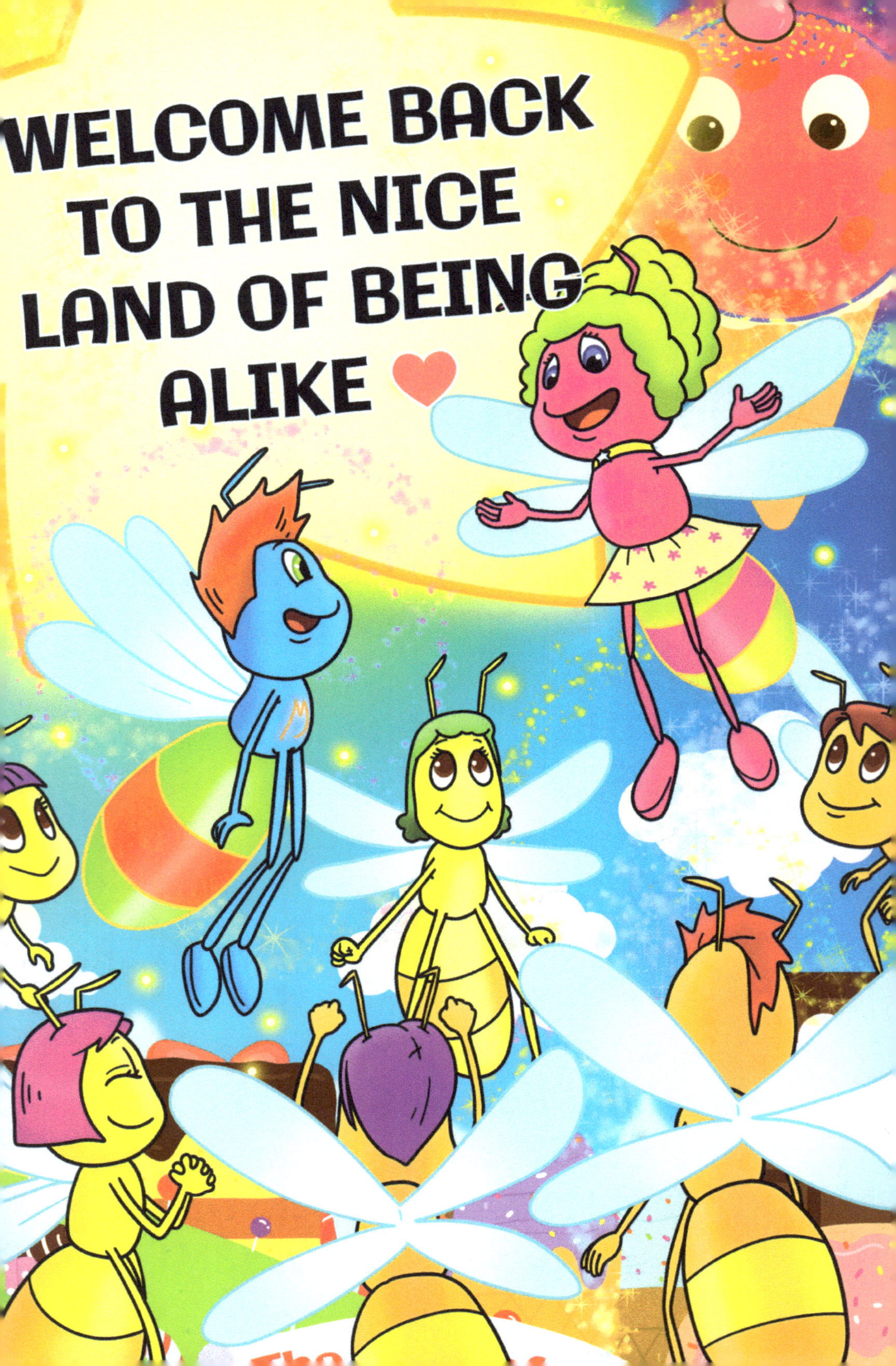

WELCOME BACK TO THE NICE LAND OF BEING ALIKE

Published by Circles Legacy Publishing LLC
Book design copyright © 2020
Project Manager and Team Coordinator Mary Cindell Lynn Pilapil
Illustrations: Patrick Bucoy
Cover design: Jim Villaflores
Layout Coordinator: Joseph Apuhin

Published in the United States of America

ISBN: xxx-x-xxxx-xxxx-x

Juvenile fiction / Fantasy and magic
Juvenile fiction / Family / General
March 06, 2020

Joslin has 16 other children books. All books are available in bookstores, Walmart online, Barnes and Noble, Amazon and other major distributors.

BUT WAIT! THERE IS SOMETHING ELSE NEW TOO. BECAUSE SOME OF THESE COOL BOOKS HAVE BEEN TURNED INTO MERRY MOVIES! For more information about new books and the animated movies that are coming along, please visit www.joslinfun.com